The Boxcar Children

THE HAUNTED CABIN MYSTERY

created by
GERTRUDE CHANDLER WARNER

Illustrated by Charles Tang

ALBERT WHITMAN & Company
Morton Grove, Illinois

ISBN 0-8075-3178-2

1 3 5 7 9 10 8 6 4 2

Printed in the U.S.A.

Contents

CHAPTER 1

The Telegram

Outside in the woods, a cool breeze stirred. Inside the boxcar, the four Alden children were hot from their hard work. Finally twelve-year-old Jessie stood up.

"Now that is what I call clean," she said, smiling at her two brothers and her ten-year-old sister, Violet.

"And neat," her older brother, Henry, said. "I'm glad you thought of this," he added, turning to Violet as she gave the pillows a final pat.

"It'll be fun to come home from an adventure and find our wonderful boxcar so shiny and nice," Benny said. "Look, even Watch is hot and tired from our work."

"Watch is a lazybones," Jessie said fondly. "He didn't do anything but watch."

"That's his job, but he loved our boxcar from the first," Violet said, smiling down at him. "Remember how we found him when we came to live here after our mother and father died? Watch is really one of us."

"Then why can't we take him on this adventure with us?" Benny asked.

"Come on, Benny," Henry said, patting his little brother. "Who ever heard of a dog traveling on a paddle-wheel boat up the Mississippi River? Anyway, Watch has stayed home to guard Grandfather's house before."

"I know," Benny said, nodding. "But I'm going to miss him anyway."

Outside, the children stretched in the cool New England air. "Now we'd better go back to Grandfather's house and pack," Henry said. Then he laughed. "Can you believe that once we ran away and hid from our own grandfather because we thought he was mean? I don't know how we could have been more wrong."

"Maybe by taking lessons," Benny said soberly, who thought a lot about lessons and school now that he was six.

Violet laughed. "Who ever heard of taking lessons to be wrong? It's more fun to learn to be right!"

Jessie said, "Grandfather says his friend Cap Lambert was a riverboat pilot for years. He knows all sorts of wonderful stories about the Mississippi River."

"And his log cabin where we'll visit is a hundred years old," Henry added. "Staying there will be a real treat."

"Cap Lambert has to be a wonderful man," Violet said, "to invite us to visit him when he hasn't even met us. I like him already."

"And I like the trip up the river to his house, too," Benny said, breaking into a run. "Let's go pack!"

That next morning their grandfather glanced at the four brightly colored suitcases in the back of the car. "I wish I could go along on this trip with you," he told them. "But business is business, and I know you'll enjoy my friend Cap."

"I hope he'll enjoy us, too," Jessie said quietly. "Didn't you say he has a son of his own?"

Mr. Alden nodded. "A very nice boy named Jason. Of course he's a grown man by now. But he and his father had a big disagreement when Jason was quite young. They haven't even seen each other for many years."

"What did they disagree about?" Jessie asked.

"Cap wanted Jason to be a doctor or lawyer. Jason only wanted to be a sailor like Cap himself," Mr. Alden replied. "Jason ran away and did what he wanted and never came back."

Benny snuggled against his grandfather. "I'm never going to leave you," he told him.

"Except for adventures," Henry put in, grinning.

"At least you'll fly with us as far as St. Louis, Grandfather," Violet said. "Will you come right back home from there?"

Mr. Alden shook his head. "I have business in the south. But I'll be in touch with you by phone. Of course, Mrs. McGregor will be here taking care of the house and Watch. I'll call and check on them, too, as I always do."

The Mississippi River was only a quick taxi ride from the St. Louis airport. Benny, holding his bright-red suitcase, stared at the huge paddle-wheel steamer.

"Did you ever see so many flags?" Violet cried. "And listen to the music!"

Her grandfather laughed. "What better way to celebrate the Fourth of July than on America's longest river?"

"And the third-longest river in the world," Jessie added. Then she smiled. "I only know that because I looked it up."

A stream of people were moving up the decorated ramp. At the top, a group of ship's officers stood waiting.

"Can you come aboard with us?" Jessie asked Mr. Alden. "Just for a while?"

"I wouldn't miss it," he said, smiling down at her. "I like being able to imagine where you are in my mind."

Henry, feeling very grown-up for fourteen, handed their tickets to the blond officer at the desk.

"Welcome aboard!" the man said, nodding at the children. Then he turned to their grandfather. "Greetings to you, too, sir. The captain's assistant asked to see you as soon as you came aboard. He has a message for you." He turned to lead the way. The children and their grandfather followed him.

A man in uniform met them as they neared his office. "This telegram arrived for you," he said. "I was asked to see that you got it before you left the ship."

The children watched their grandfather's face as he read the telegram. When he frowned, Benny slid his hand into Henry's.

Mr. Alden looked up and put his arm across Jessie's shoulders. "Thank you again," he told the ship's officer. "I need a quiet place to talk to my children for a moment."

"You're welcome to my office," the man said. "I'm needed on deck."

When the door closed behind him, Mr. Alden looked around at the children. "This is disappointing news," he said. "It's from Cap. Let me read it to you."

"Dear Friend. Stop," Mr. Alden read. "I can't tell you how unhappy I am to write this. Stop. I have looked forward very much to having your fine children here. Stop. But I have to ask you not to send them due to an injury to my ankle that makes me unable to get around. Stop. Regards always. Cap Lambert."

"Why does he keep telling you to stop?" Benny cried. "We don't want to stop. We want to go there."

His grandfather chuckled. "That's just the way telegrams are written. Stop is like a period. Poor Cap! I know he hates having to call off your visit. I'm sure that he's just as disappointed as you children are."

"Oh, but, Grandfather," Jessie said. "If he's having trouble getting around, that's an even better reason for us to go. We can take care of him and help him with his work. Remember what a good nurse Violet is? And we can see that he eats right so his ankle will heal. Didn't you say that he lives all alone?"

"Except for his pet rooster, Doodle," Benny put in.

"Jessie's right," Henry said. "Your friend doesn't know that we have the best time if we have real things to do."

Their grandfather listened thoughtfully.

"You see, Grandfather," Henry said, "your friend doesn't know us. He thinks *he'll* have to take care of *us*. Instead, *we* can take care of *him*. And we'd really like to do it."

Mr. Alden hesitated, still looking doubtful. "He won't be expecting you when the boat reaches Hannibal," he pointed out. "There'll be no one there to meet you and take you out to his place. His cabin is at least three miles from town."

"We've had worse problems than that," Henry reminded him. "Remember the time we got snowbound in a cabin? The store was almost that far away from us."

Violet took her grandfather's hand and

looked up into his face. "Don't you know that we like doing things for people more than anything?" she asked. "Surely he won't mind our coming if he knows how much we *want* to help."

Mr. Alden smiled and caught the four of them against him in a big hug. "You win, and so does Cap. I'll call him from shore and let him know you're coming. And I'll depend on you, as always, to come through with flying colors."

Within minutes, they were waving from the deck to the tall, white-haired man who saluted them from shore.

CHAPTER 2

The Double Celebration

The boys got their unpacking done before the girls had finished. "Now can we go and explore?" Benny asked, almost jumping up and down with excitement.

"Go on ahead," Violet told him. "We're almost through. We'll meet you up on deck."

The cabins were small and shining clean, with two bunk beds in each one. Violet and Jessie unpacked the clothes they would wear on the boat and hung them in a tiny metal closet. After they finished, they went up on deck to look for Henry and Benny.

One of the ship's officers was going up the narrow stairs in front of them. "Excuse me, sir," Jessie said. "Have you seen two boys — a tall one and a short one — come this way?"

The man only glanced at them before looking away so his face was half hidden. Then he nodded. "I believe you'll find the Alden boys on the top deck," he said with no warmth in his voice.

Violet looked back as she and Jessie climbed the narrow stairs. "How did he know our last name?" she wondered aloud.

"I saw him checking our names off a list when Henry handed in our tickets," Jessie said. "He looked at Grandfather and us very strangely then."

"That's the second strange thing about that Mr. Jay," Violet said thoughtfully.

Jessie looked at the man who was disappearing into the crowd. Then she laughed. "Now *you* are being mysterious. How did you know his name? And what was the second strange thing about him?"

In spite of Jessie's teasing, Violet didn't

even smile. "His name is written on that gold-colored pin he's wearing," Violet said. "And didn't you notice how he wouldn't look us in the face? It was almost as if he didn't want us to see what he looked like."

Jessie nodded. "You're right. He's not at all friendly."

Then they were at the top of the stairs. The boys were at the rail looking up at a huge bridge spanning the river.

"I wonder when we're going to leave," Benny asked. "I want to see the paddle wheel turn."

One of the ship's officers turned and smiled down at him. "First we'll have dinner and let it get dark," he told Benny. "You want to see the fireworks, don't you?"

"Oh, yes," Benny said. Then he grinned at the man. "But I'm not sure which I like best, dinner or fireworks."

Their first meal on board was served on long tables where they all could take what they wanted. Violet's eyes widened at the huge table of beautiful food. She filled her plate with melon and strawberries, along with chicken, cheese and bread. Benny tried to take at least some of everything, but Jessie talked him into stopping when he started piling on the second layer.

When they went back up on deck, a tall man with a red mustache and glasses was standing by the rail. "Here," he said, stepping aside to make room for them. "Take my place. I can see over your heads."

Henry thanked him, then stared up at the bridge that crossed the river. "What a great bridge," he said.

The man nodded. "It's called the Eads Bridge," he said. "It was built back in the nineteenth century."

Jessie looked at him and smiled. "You must read a lot to know things like that."

He smiled. "I do," he said. "But it's my business, too. I write articles for newspapers. I'm always looking for interesting things to write about. I'm Paul Edwards. If you're the Alden children, we'll be having meals together. I saw your names on my table list."

"Look," Benny cried, pointing back toward the city. Fireworks had begun to explode above the tall buildings of St. Louis. Rockets and bright flashes rose into the sky on both sides of the river.

"I wish Grandfather could see this," Violet whispered.

Benny was leaning against Henry by the time the fireworks ended in a giant burst of color that filled the sky. The ship began to move. "I'm thirsty," Benny said, his voice suddenly sad. "And I just remembered that I forgot something important."

Jessie laughed and opened her bag. "It couldn't be this, could it?" she asked, handing him the pink cup he had kept ever since finding it in the dump when they lived in the boxcar.

He smiled, taking it from her with both hands. "Thank you, Jessie," he said softly, his voice happy again.

She hugged him. "Now what do you say we go to bed so we'll all be perky tomorrow?"

"If you say so," he said. "But I'm not at

all sleepy." He grinned at himself when a wide yawn caught him right in the middle of his words.

Mr. Edwards was right. He was assigned to their table along with some other friendly people. They all agreed that bacon and eggs had never tasted better than that morning.

Up on deck, they watched a tiny tugboat moving upstream, pushing a huge barge of lumber past them. The sailors on the tug shouted and waved their caps at the children as they passed. Jessie looked down and saw Mr. Jay watching them from the deck below. The minute he saw her looking at him, he turned on his heel and walked away.

"We have a mystery man," Jessie whispered to Henry.

"What's the mystery about him?" Henry asked.

"His name is Mr. Jay, and no matter where we are, I see him staring at us," she said. "But the minute I look at *him*, he gets away as fast as he can. It's almost as if he were spying on us but didn't want us to know it."

"He never smiles," Violet added. "And he's the only man on the ship who isn't really polite to us."

Henry frowned. "That *is* mysterious," he said. "Be sure to point him out to me the next time you see him."

That night after sunset, Mr. Edwards led them to the very top of the boat where the pilots worked. "See how they play those beams of light across the water in front of us?" he asked.

"What would happen without them?" Jessie asked.

"The boat could get stuck on a sandbar," he said, "and have to be pushed off. In the old days, outlaws often lurked along the river. Sometimes they came aboard and robbed people."

"Like pirates?" Benny asked. "I know about pirates."

Mr. Edwards nodded. "About the same," he said. "Wolf Island up ahead was well known for the bad men who hid there to attack passing boats."

"Do you write about things like this in your articles?" Jessie asked.

He nodded. "I just published a story about a half a million dollars in gold coins that's supposed to be buried up there south of Hannibal in one of those valleys."

"That's where we're going," Benny told him, practically bouncing out of his chair.

Mr. Edwards laughed. "Stories of buried treasure never seem to die away, but nobody ever finds any gold, either."

There was so much to see and do that the day passed quickly.

After Jessie and Violet pointed out Mr. Jay to the boys, Henry agreed that he seemed to be everywhere.

"Like outlaws along the river," Benny said.

"Well, not exactly," Henry laughed, but he wondered. Why would a stranger like that be spying on them and then act as if he were afraid they would recognize him?

"Have any of you ever seen this Mr. Jay anywhere before we got on board?" Henry asked.

"Never," they agreed, shaking their heads.

Before they knew it, the ship was being towed to shore at Hannibal. Jessie sighed. "This was such fun that I hate to see it end."

They said good-bye to Mr. Edwards and thanked him for his wonderful stories. Then, their suitcases in hand, they streamed off the boat with the other passengers.

CHAPTER 3

Cap and Doodle

After they left the ship, the children decided that they needed to call Cap Lambert the very first thing.

"Can I just sit some place and wait?" Benny asked. "My legs feel funny when I walk."

"Mine do, too," Jessie said. "Those are our 'sea legs.' We'll get our land legs back right away."

The girls and Benny sat on a bench while Henry went to use a public phone. They were barely settled before he was back. "Cap

Lambert's phone has been disconnected," he said, frowning thoughtfully.

"Oh, that's not good at all," Violet said. "If he's been injured, he needs a phone."

"And it means that Grandfather wasn't able to call him to say we were on the boat. He must not even know we're coming," Henry said. "It's not very nice just to surprise him."

"I know he'll be glad when he sees us," Benny said. "Grandfather said it was only three miles to his house. That's not very far for us to walk."

"You're right, Benny," Jessie said. "But remember, Cap Lambert has been hurt. If he isn't expecting us, he may not be prepared. I think we should take some groceries."

Benny jumped up. "That's a *great* idea," he said. "They had everything I liked on the ship except peanut butter."

"Do you have your land legs back?" Jessie asked.

Benny nodded and raced into the store to prove it. The grocer watched them with interest as they picked out things they all liked. Along with the regular groceries, like dried milk, cocoa, spaghetti, and tomato sauce, they bought some treats — cinnamon candy, marshmallows, and, of course, peanut butter, a large jar. While the grocer added up their bill, Henry picked up a lamp and looked at it. It had a funny smell.

"That's a kerosene lamp," the grocer told him. "They come in mighty handy where there isn't any electricity." He looked at the bags of groceries and frowned. "Surely you're not aiming to carry all this clear out to Lambert's?"

"There are four of us," Henry reminded him.

"No matter," he said. "I might find you a ride with somebody going that way."

The children looked at each other, then Jessie smiled at him. "That's very nice of you," she said. "But we like walking. But we need to know the way to find Owl's Glen."

A little later, as they set off with a suitcase in one hand and a bag of groceries in the other, Henry spoke quietly. "Look back," he said. "Isn't that Mr. Jay watching us there by the post office?"

Jessie glanced back, nodding. "You're right," she said.

"Where?" Violet asked. But by the time she turned, he had turned away and disappeared down the side street.

"I don't like it when people spy on us and I don't know why," Benny said.

"None of us do," Jessie told him. "But we won't have to wonder about him any more. Our boat will go back down the river to St. Louis this afternoon. He'll be on it, and we'll probably never see him again."

"I do like mysteries, though," Benny admitted.

The road to Cap Lambert's was mostly downhill. Tall bushes and trees grew close to its side, shutting off the light. The road crossed a stream that was marked POSSUM CREEK. By the time they saw a log cabin up ahead, it was getting dark.

"Do you suppose that's Cap's place?" Jessie asked, stopping. The chimney of the low cabin sent a thin wisp of blue smoke into the sky. The giant pine trees cast such a deep shade that the cabin's porch was in full darkness.

"I don't hear any owls," Benny said, setting down his suitcase and groceries. "But let's stop and see anyway. My legs are tired of this road. It sure is dark here. Maybe the cabin is haunted."

Jessie laughed. "Benny! What an imagination you have."

As Henry unlocked the gate, a sudden screeching came from the porch. With a flash of red and a beating of wings, a brightly colored rooster flew squawking down the walk at them. Benny yipped with delight and ran to meet the rooster.

"Doodle," Benny cried, kneeling, forgetting his fears.

The rooster stopped with his wings still spread. As he cocked his head at Benny, a gruff voice came from the porch. "Get back here, Doodle, you crazy rooster. What's going on out there, anyway?"

Before anyone could answer, Benny had run up to the porch. "You must be Cap Lambert," he said in a rush. "How did you get hurt, anyway? I hope you're feeling better."

"What is this?" the old man asked, peering at him from the shade. "Go away, whoever you are."

The girls looked at each other with wide eyes as Henry stepped forward to join Benny. "We're the Alden children," he said.

The man on the porch was sitting in a high-backed chair. His bandaged leg was propped on a stool. A pair of crutches leaned against the wall. He looked terribly old in the dim light. His gray hair stuck out under his cap, and his full curling beard was gray, too. "I guess my message didn't reach you. That's a pity."

"Oh, but it did!" Benny said. "We came anyway."

The rooster had come back up the walk. He flapped up to sit on Cap's shoulder and stare at the children.

"You must be Benny," Cap Lambert said. "Your grandfather told me you were a talker."

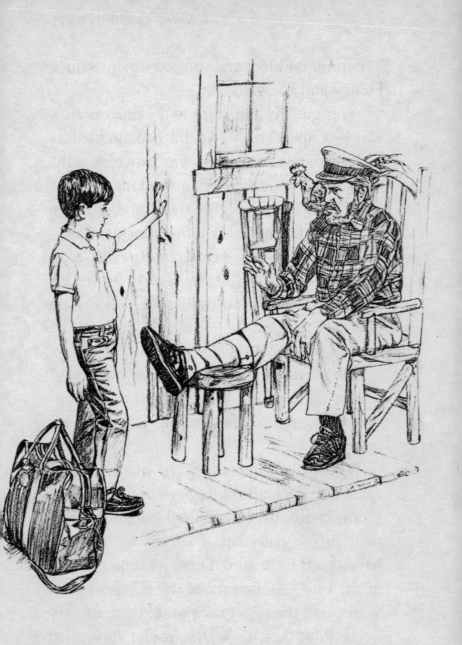

Benny nodded and turned to introduce Henry and the girls.

"You got my telegram and came on anyway?" Cap asked when he had nodded at each of the children. He was frowning a little. "What was that Alden thinking of?"

"It was our idea," Jessie admitted. "We had to talk Grandfather into letting us come."

"You should have saved your breath," Cap Lambert grumbled. "I'll have to turn you around and send you right back. There's no one here to care for you, and it's not safe around here anyway."

"Oh, but we came to take care of *you*," Violet said, telling him how they had convinced their grandfather. He listened, still frowning.

"You make a fair case," he finally admitted. "I've been afraid to go out on the rough ground with this bad ankle. I called the mailman in to send that telegram for me and haven't left the cabin. There was enough feed in the bins to take care of the chickens for a while, and the eggs can wait in the nests. My horse Pilot gets his water from a spring-fed trough and has plenty of hay. The garden and orchard just have to tend themselves."

"We're good with chickens," Benny told him. "And horses, too. We learned out on Aunt Jane's ranch."

Cap looked at them and sighed. "There's nothing to do tonight, I guess. You might as well take your things inside. We'll worry about getting you back to town tomorrow. I suppose you're hungry, too."

"I'm always hungry," Benny told him, grinning.

"But you don't have to worry about food," Jessie said quickly. "All of us like to cook, and we brought things for dinner. Henry and I will fix it while Benny and Violet help you inside."

Jessie's plan worked perfectly. By the time Cap was installed in his rocking chair by the hearth, the water was boiling for spaghetti, and tomato sauce was simmering on the back of the old wood stove. Violet found a red-and-white-checkered cloth for the round oak table and went outside to look for some flowers for a centerpiece. As she picked a bunch of wild daisies at the edge of the woods, she heard a kitten mew. She stood very still, looking for it, but she never did find it.

Cap Lambert sniffed the air and winked at Benny. "I believe I'm as hungry as you are, Benny," he said. "I've been getting along on cold things I could rustle for myself."

Even though the cabin needed a good cleaning, it looked cozy and friendly with the five of them gathered around the table.

"We were all sorry to hear you were hurt," Henry said. "Tell us about your accident."

Cap Lambert's voice had lost its gruffness as they made friends. His color was better, too, after eating two heaping plates of hot spaghetti. But his voice sounded worried as he tried to explain. "That was the strangest thing ever. I know every inch of this place with my eyes shut. There never had been any deep hole out there by the garden before. But there I was with my foot down in it and my ankle twisted under me. It hurt too much to do anything but hobble back inside. By morning that ankle was as big around as my head, and I've been laid up ever since."

"Are you sure it's not broken?" Violet asked, looking at him with concern.

He nodded. "I can move my foot around. It's just too sprained and swollen to walk on. That's why I asked the mailman to send that telegram to your grandfather."

"That's not enough reason to keep us away," Henry said. "We'll have fun taking care of you and your place."

"But I had other reasons besides that to keep you from coming," Cap said, his voice getting lower and angry again. "Things just aren't the same around here anymore. I feel too far from everybody, and strange things happen that I don't understand, like a hole coming in the ground overnight."

"You must have neighbors," Jessie said.

"I used to," he said. "But just this spring my neighbor Roger Hodges got killed in a car accident. There're only his wife and children left over the hill, and I haven't seen Susie or Ned since summer came." He looked up at Jessie. "I miss those kids. Susie's about your size, I'd guess, and Ned has just turned ten."

"Like me," Violet said, rising to clear the table. Then she paused and glanced over at Doodle, perched on the back of Cap's chair. "Do you have a cat?" she asked Cap.

He looked up and shook his head. "Never in this life," he said. "Why do you ask?"

She smiled. "I was sure I heard a kitten out in your yard. I couldn't find it. But a bird flew out of that same bush. It couldn't have been a bird, could it?"

He laughed. "I'm not much on birds, but I'd say it was a strange bird that would make the noise of a cat."

CHAPTER 4

Weird Noises, Strange Lights

Benny finished the last of the milk in his pink cup and handed it to Violet. He frowned, still thinking about Cap's accident. "You might feel closer to people if you had your telephone fixed," he said.

"I had that thing disconnected myself," Cap told him crossly. "I was getting calls that didn't make any sense. That phone would ring and when I'd answer it, no one would say anything. I knew there was somebody there because I could hear breathing."

Henry and Jessie exchanged glances. Why

would anyone call Cap up and then just breathe?

"I must say it's nice to have your company tonight," Cap went on. "But I'll get you into the hotel in town tomorrow. You'll be safe there until your grandfather comes."

"We've had lots of adventures alone," Benny protested.

Cap nodded, but his frown didn't go away.

Cap was no housekeeper. Although the house had electricity and running water, it was otherwise very simple. Jessie finally found a dishpan and a drying rack. When Henry came to help her and Violet with the dishes, she shook her head. "Maybe you and Violet should check things outside. The chickens will be asleep, but you might check on the horse."

Cap nodded. "I would appreciate your checking on Pilot," he said. "He's probably lonesome and would like a pan of oats."

When Violet and Henry came back from the barn, the tiny kitchen was shining. "My, you are good workers," Cap said. "Everything's done, and it's too early to go to bed."

Then he chuckled. "How about you make us up a big bowl of popcorn? We can take it out on the porch and get better acquainted."

Benny clapped his hands. "I love popcorn," he said.

"So does Doodle," Cap told him. "That's why I haven't made any since I hurt my ankle. He can eat it faster than I can get it off the cob and into the pan. I'll tell you where it is, and we'll take this rascal outside until it's done."

The children had never seen popcorn still on the dry cob. Jessie shelled it while Henry heated the heavy pan on the stove. Within minutes the popcorn was exploding under the pot lid while Henry shook it to keep it from burning.

"I've never eaten popcorn this good," Violet said when they were settled on the dark porch. "Where do you get it on a cob like this?"

Cap's laugh was warm and rich. "I grow it right out there in my own garden."

"I love gardening," Jessie said. "Tomorrow I'll go see if it needs weeding."

The crickets sang in the darkness as Cap told them about his life as a riverboat pilot. The children told Cap about their friend from the boat, Paul Edwards. He nodded. "There're a million and one stories about that river to keep a writer going," he said. "I believe I recognize that name."

Benny, leaning against Jessie on the steps, fell asleep, dropping his bowl and spilling the last kernels of corn.

"Doodle is dead asleep for the night," Cap laughed, "or he'd be after that corn in a minute. Let's turn in. This night has been a rare treat for me. Who would have thought you kids could be such a big help?"

Doodle had his head under one wing on Cap's shoulder.

"Where does Doodle sleep?" Violet asked.

Cap looked a little embarrassed. "He has a cage in my room. I've kept him there since I was hurt. While the foxes can't get into the chicken yard if the gate is closed, the hawks can fly in. I was afraid he might get carried off. If I cover his cage, he doesn't crow until I get up."

Cap's small cabin was cozy. The living room with its giant fireplace, Cap's bedroom, and the kitchen formed the main part of the house. The children were to sleep on the screened porch that ran clear across the back. Jessie and Violet had narrow but comfortable cots at one end, with Henry's and Benny's at the other.

As they climbed into their cots, Violet asked Jessie, "Do you think he means to let us stay?"

Jessie laughed softly. "We just need to be so helpful that he can't spare us. Let's see who can do the most useful things."

"And who can solve the mystery, too," Benny said. "*Holes* just don't dig themselves, you know."

"You're right," Henry said. "Here we were hoping for one mystery and we get a whole bunch of them. Telephones don't ring and breathe without someone else on the line, either."

"But who would do a thing like that?" Jessie asked.

"And why would they want to?" Violet

added. "Well, we need to find a whole lot of things if we're going to help Cap." Violet dropped her head on her pillow. "For that, I need a good night's sleep."

Once the lights were out, Jessie fell asleep almost instantly along with the others. When the strange sound wakened her, she sat up, startled. Violet stirred and whispered something in her sleep, but the boys slept on.

With her quilt around her shoulders, Jessie went to the window to stare out into the woods. The barn was a larger shadow against the uneven darkness beyond. She listened to the noisy darkness, the droning of insects, and the thumping of frogs. The sound that had wakened her was different, but more like a whistle than a birdcall. She had never heard a birdcall anything like that.

She was still trying to figure out what it could have been when she saw the light moving back among the trees. Could someone be out there with a flashlight? She saw it shine weakly, then disappear to a glow again a few yards away. It was always at the same height. She tiptoed to Henry's side. He woke up at

her touch and whispered, "What's wrong?"

Jessie signaled him to silence and pointed to the woods. He sat up and stared out as she had done. When the light appeared, he caught her arm, whispering, "What is it?"

"I don't know," she said. Finally the light disappeared behind the barn.

"That's weird," Henry whispered. "I can't figure out how you could make a light move like that unless someone was carrying it."

"That makes it scary," Jessie said. "Nobody has any business out there at night."

"Maybe Cap would know what it was," Henry said thoughtfully.

Jessie shook her head. "I don't think we should say anything about it. He's already too nervous. Remember how he looked when he told us about hurting himself — in a hole that hadn't been there before? And those spooky telephone calls? If he thought any more strange things were going on, I'm sure he'd make us go stay in town."

"You're probably right," Henry agreed. "Tomorrow we'll all go explore out there. We're sure to find some clues."

CHAPTER 5

Will-o'-the-Wisp

When Jessie woke up again, she heard a lot of different sounds. The horse whinnied in the barn as Henry talked to it. She heard the chickens fussing in their yard, and a noise like a kitten crying "Mew" over and over. Violet was in the kitchen putting on water to make coffee for Cap.

"What a good idea," Jessie told her. "Cap probably wants coffee first thing, just like Grandfather does. Oh, and I wanted to tell you. I heard a kitten cry, too."

"We'll keep watching for it," Violet said.

Jessie nodded in agreement. "Now, what can we cook?"

"I found a ham bone in the refrigerator," Violet told her. "I've cut off a bowlful of little pieces. If there are eggs out there, we could have an omelet with toast and jam."

"Wonderful!" Jessie said. "There's a wire basket hanging on the porch. I'll go look for eggs."

She found eggs in every nest, altogether a dozen plus two. Henry, coming from the barn, opened the back door for her to carry them inside.

The ham sizzling in the skillet and the rich coffee smell brought Cap swinging out of his room on his crutches. Doodle rode on his left shoulder. "I've never smelled anything as good as this morning," he said, peering at the ham before he sat down. "Was there really that much meat on that bone?"

"Sure was," Violet told him. "With enough left over for soup." She smiled at him. As she spoke, she whipped six eggs in a bowl with a fork, then added them to the ham.

"I hope that Susie and little Ned are getting on as well as you do," Cap said. "They have their mother, at least."

"Don't they ever come over to see you?" Benny asked.

"Not these past months," Cap told him. "They must be visiting grandparents off somewhere. I miss them, too."

The omelet had been divided up and was half eaten when Benny looked at Cap. "What was that funny light I saw out in the woods last night?" he asked.

"Lightning bugs?" Cap asked.

Jessie and Henry exchanged glances. So much for keeping the strange lights a secret from Cap!

"It didn't dance. It flickered," Benny said.

Cap's face darkened, and his voice sounded doubtful. "There's such a thing as a will-o'-the-wisp," he said. "They say it flickers in marshy places."

"Will-o'-the-wisp!" Violet cried. "I love that name."

Cap shook his head, looking very grumpy. "If you're seeing such strange lights as that,

I don't want you stepping out of this house after dark. You hear?"

The children nodded and went back to their breakfast. But Jessie caught Henry's eye. Any mention of strange things upset Cap. She was sorry Benny had seen the light. They needed to solve these strange little mysteries fast so the old man's mind could be put at ease.

When the breakfast dishes were done, the four children told Cap that they wanted to explore his little farm. The garden was just beyond the barn with the orchard on the far side of that. Suddenly Henry, who was still prowling around the barn, called to the others. "Come look," he said. "I want you to see something."

Jessie and Violet ran to him at once. "Isn't this about where we saw the flickering light last night?" he asked.

"It looks right to me," Jessie said, looking around for Benny, who had seen it, too.

"Where did Benny go?" Henry asked.

"He was with us in the garden," Violet

said, looking back. When Benny didn't answer Jessie's call, they all three ran toward the woods, calling his name.

Suddenly his little round face appeared above them from the dense foliage of an oak tree. "Here I am," Benny cried happily. "I found a squirrel house."

Henry went to the foot of the tree and looked up. "Squirrels don't have houses, Benny," he said. "They have nests. Where are you, anyway? I can't see you."

"Right up here. Come see for yourself," Benny called. "This house is full of nut shells like squirrels leave, and a lot of trash. Oh," he said suddenly, "and a fire truck."

Violet frowned. Henry was right. Squirrels lived in nests instead of houses, and they didn't play with fire trucks, either. "I want to see, too," she called up to Benny.

Henry had already shinnied out of sight up into the tree. "Be careful," he called down to his sisters. "There is a tree house up here, but the wood is old and rotten."

Soon they were all crammed into the little

house. Its roof was slanted with holes cut out for windows. "Isn't it great?" Benny asked. "And look!"

He held up a tiny metal fire truck with only three wheels and most of the red paint worn off. Violet turned the little truck in her hand. She said quietly, "I'm sure that this tree house belonged to Cap's son Jason. And this must be his fire truck. Cap must have loved his son very much to make him such a nice playhouse. He must still miss him a lot, too."

"But he's never once mentioned him," Jessie said.

"Maybe it hurts Cap to think about him," Henry said.

"Can I take the fire truck?" Benny asked, holding the toy tightly in his hand.

Henry looked at his sisters. "I think it would be all right if you don't let Cap see it," Violet said. "Seeing it would only remind him and make him feel even more sad."

"I could stay up here forever," Benny said. "I love this place."

"It *is* great," Henry agreed, "but Cap will worry if we're gone too long."

"What were you going to show us back by the barn?" Jessie asked Henry. "Did you find a clue there?"

"Not exactly a clue," he said, leading them to a place near the end of the barn. "I just wanted to show you something. This is where we saw the light. Right?"

When Jessie and Benny nodded, he told them to feel the ground. "Why, it's as dry as an old bone," Jessie said.

"Then we can't have seen a will-o'-the-wisp as Cap suggested. That only happens on wet marshy ground," Henry reminded them. "We saw something else flickering out here."

"You're right," Jessie said. "And Violet and I found something really confusing in the garden, too. Cap said he hasn't been out in his garden since his accident."

"But everything is perfect out there," Violet added. "The beans and tomatoes look as if they have been picked every day. The carrots have even been thinned, and none of the spinach has gone to seed."

The children stared at each other. "Do squirrels and possums eat vegetables?" Benny asked.

"They do," Henry said, "but they just bite chunks out. Only a person would thin carrots and spinach."

"But who?" Jessie asked. "There's no one around here. There's not even a house close by."

Henry shook his head. "The more we look for answers, the more questions we get," he said. "Let's not upset Cap more by telling him about this. What do you say?"

Benny nodded. "His ankle never will get well if he just swings around on those crutches all the time being worried."

Violet made soup with the ham bone and vegetables. It smelled so good that everyone wanted to eat early. The boys made popcorn, which they all ate out on the porch.

That night before going to sleep, the children held another whispered conversation. "We can't go another day without getting in touch with Grandfather," Jessie said. "If he doesn't hear from us, he might get worried. He might even think he has to come get us."

"Oh, he mustn't!" Violet cried. "Cap really needs us. And we can't leave here until we solve these mysteries."

Benny, lying in bed on his stomach, said, "Just call home and tell Mrs. McGregor. Grandfather is always in touch with her. And be sure to ask how Watch is, too."

Jessie grinned. Benny always had a good plan. And she didn't mind that he thought of Watch as *his* dog even though he really belonged to Jessie herself.

"I'll call Grandfather. Who wants to walk along with me to town?" Henry asked. "I need to buy some other things, too."

"I'd love to go," Violet said. "We've got plenty of soup left over for lunch, and we'd be back for supper."

"Check the peanut butter before you go," Benny mumbled drowsily.

CHAPTER 6

Scrambled Eggs

Violet woke up just before dawn. She dressed silently, thinking of what would taste the best for breakfast. She decided on French toast with honey.

She took down the egg basket, wishing the sun would come up faster. The minute she stepped outside, things began to happen. The chickens began squawking, and a small dog she'd never seen before darted past her. She gasped as she looked after him. For a minute she was tempted to run back inside until it was light. But that was silly. She'd never been afraid of the dark. What harm could come from a reddish-looking little dog with a plumed tail?

She couldn't see a thing as she slid her hand into the warm nests and felt for eggs. When she had emptied all the nests, she had eight eggs. She stood still, frowning.

This was curious. Jessie had found fourteen eggs the day before. If the chickens laid eight eggs every day, Jessie should have found a lot more than fourteen eggs. What had happened to the eggs the hens had laid before they got there? Cap said he hadn't gathered them since he got hurt.

Violet shook her head. This really was a strange place! The other mysteries they'd solved hadn't been like this. None of these puzzling things seemed to have anything to do with each other.

She was about to leave the henhouse when a low, strange whistle sent an icy shiver up her back. The piercing sound was so close that her breath came short. Was this the same noise Jessie had heard? For the first time Violet was truly scared! Before the sound even died away, something went crashing off into the bushes. It sounded like an animal — a *big* animal. For a moment, she couldn't move.

She took a deep breath. As she stepped out into the darkness, she saw something disappearing into the trees. It was still too dark to see it clearly. It looked lumpy and black and was bent over. The funny way it ran made it even scarier. She knew it wasn't a bear, but she couldn't think of what else it *could* be. Whatever it was scared her so much that she forgot all about her basket of eggs and ran for the cabin.

She was almost to the back porch when Cap came around the side of the house on his crutches. Violet must have looked as scared as she felt because he stared at her a minute. Then he said, "Violet, what's wrong?" Before she could answer, he motioned her to follow him. "Come on, my dear. Come around to the porch with me."

Violet looked down at her egg basket and gasped. Broken eggs were pouring out between the wires of the basket in a golden stream. "Never mind that," Cap said impatiently. "Come along with me. You can tend to those eggs later."

She followed him with a thundering heart. What had she done to make him sound so cross? Once into his chair, he looked up at her, still frowning. "I want to know exactly what scared you out there," he said in a stern voice. When she couldn't think of how to answer right away, he went on impatiently. "Was it a whistling?"

She nodded. "An awful whistling, and a red dog, and something running off into the brush."

He frowned. "The chickens woke me up," he said. "Did you see anything like a hawk around the henhouse?"

"Only that little red dog," she told him. She had seen that other thing, but she couldn't possibly describe it.

"Did it have a sharp nose and a big plume of a tail?"

"I didn't see its face, but its tail was bushy."

He sighed. "That was no dog, Violet.

That was a fox. Foxes and hawks both rob chicken houses and carry off hens. How many hens do I have out there now?"

"I never thought to count them," she admitted.

He glanced at the morning light that was flooding into the clearing. "Would you mind going to see how many there are?" he asked. "You won't be scared, will you?"

She shook her head and ran back to the henhouse. She counted the hens twice to be sure she had the number right.

"Eleven," she told Cap when she got back to the porch. "All snow white."

He stared at her. "No red hen at all?"

She shook her head, "All white."

He sighed. "That's worse than I feared. When I got hurt, I had eleven white Plymouth Rock hens and a beautiful Rhode Island red hen named Rhoda. She was my special pet, and Doodle's, too. Although it sounded strange, that whistle we heard may have been a hawk or an eagle." He shook his head. "We'll miss poor Rhoda. But thank you, Violet. I'm glad I didn't risk losing Doodle by leaving him out there. He's been my best friend since our old dog died. But you still must have found a lot of eggs."

"Not too many," she admitted. "Jessie found fourteen yesterday, and I only found eight today."

He frowned. "That's not near enough eggs. I tell you, Violet, strange things are going on around here. If you children weren't such good company, I'd get you into the safety of town if I had to walk you there on these crutches."

She smiled at him. "We don't want to go until you're well. But I'd better see how many of those eggs I ruined."

Two eggs were completely broken and had spilled out on the ground. Five others were so badly cracked that she had to empty them into a bowl to save them.

Cap's coffee was ready when Henry came in and looked into the bowl. "Scrambled eggs today?" he asked.

"I cracked these," Violet told him. She started telling him about the whistle and the running figure. Jessie and Benny came in from the porch to listen.

"That sounds like a dwarf out of a book," Benny said.

She stared at him. "That's exactly what it looked like, all dark and hunched over and running in that strange way. All I could think of was a bear, but it wasn't that big."

"It woke me up making a scraping noise out there," Benny said. "I heard the same noise the night we saw that funny light. It comes and goes, then comes and goes again. Remember when we got here, I said maybe the house was haunted."

Before they could ask Benny any more, Cap appeared.

Henry smiled at him and changed the subject quickly. "You're just in time for coffee," he said. "With breakfast coming right up."

When Cap was settled with his coffee, Henry went back to the stove. "You do the eggs, Violet, and I'll make French toast," he said. "Big breakfast for a big day!"

Cap and Benny both groaned when they

had finished off plates of buttery scrambled eggs and golden French toast covered with honey. "I'm glad I'm not walking into town with you," Benny said. "I'm so full I'd have to waddle."

Cap looked at him. "What's this about a trip to town?"

"Violet and I need to go to town and call home," Henry told him. "Grandfather checks with our housekeeper. He'll get the message and know we're here and having a fine time."

Cap shook his head. "No man ever had more thoughtful children than you four. You could ride Pilot into town and back."

"Could we?" Henry asked. "That would be wonderful!"

"But I want to ride the horse, too," Benny said.

"Then you go in my place," Violet said quickly. "I'll give you the grocery list Jessie and I made."

"Are you sure you don't care?" Benny asked, looking concerned.

Violet leaned to touch his shoulder. "I'll go next time."

Pilot held very still as Henry put the harness over his head. "He looks happy to be going for a ride," Violet said. "He's probably been lonely, too, like Cap."

Benny crossed the barn floor carrying a saddle blanket when he suddenly fell with a thud and yelped with pain.

"What happened?" Jessie asked, kneeling beside him.

Benny blinked to hold back his tears and hugged his right knee with both arms. "I tripped and fell," he said.

"No wonder you tripped," Henry said, kneeling beside him. "A big board has come loose under this hay."

Benny, up on his feet, stared down at it. "Look, there's a deep hole underneath it," he said. The children gathered around to examine the hollow place where the earth had been dug away under the barn floor.

"How could that have happened with the barn all closed up?" Jessie asked. "Holes have

to be dug! And they're dangerous," she added. "Someone could get hurt."

"Cap has already," Benny reminded her.

"But he didn't fall here in the barn," Violet reminded him. "He was outside, over by the water trough. He told me."

"Come look here," Jessie called. "I found another board loose, and still another one. And all of them were hidden under the hay with big holes dug underneath."

Henry stood silently for a moment, frowning as he tried to solve the puzzle. "We need to figure out what made these holes."

"Or *who* made them," Benny said, still rubbing his knee.

CHAPTER 7

The Cat Bird

The girls left Cap and Doodle dozing on the front porch. Violet climbed a tree and handed the apples down to Jessie. When her bucket was half full, Jessie stepped back and fell flat, her apples rolling off in all directions. "What happened?" Violet asked. "Are you all right?"

Jessie looked up from the ground. "There are holes all around here. They're like those at the barn except these have soft dirt thrown back in them so you can't see them."

Violet climbed down and helped gather up

the apples. Then, they walked around and found over a dozen holes. "I thought Cap was just nervous," Jessie said on the way back to the house. "Now I'm feeling nervous myself."

Violet nodded. "I wasn't nervous this morning, I was scared. I like mysteries to make better sense than this."

"Me, too," Jessie said. "We have all questions but no answers."

Back in the kitchen, Jessie sorted the apples. She kept the perfect ones for eating. She and Violet peeled the others for cooking. Violet sang happily as she got out lard and flour and salt.

"What are you going to make?" Jessie asked.

"A surprise apple pie," Violet said.

"That's a wonderful idea," Jessie said, looking doubtful. "I've looked everywhere and can't find a pie pan anywhere. I did find a lot of books stacked behind the roasting pan."

The girls looked at each other and laughed. "That's just *too* strange. Now how can I bake a pie without a tin?"

"How about turnovers or dumplings?" Jessie asked.

"Dumplings," Violet cried. "With raisins and cinnamon."

When her dumplings were bubbling in the oven, Violet took her turn at stirring the simmering applesauce. Jessie began to read one of the books. When the applesauce was done, she took the book with her as they joined Cap and Doodle on the porch.

"Look!" Jessie said. "I found the bird that makes the noise like a kitten. It is called a catbird or a Missouri mockingbird. I even found a picture of it."

"Let me see," Cap asked, reaching for the book. "I declare, you're right, Jessie. This picture is exactly like the bird Violet described."

"I've never heard of a catbird before," Violet said.

"Listen to what it says here," Cap said, reading aloud from the book. "It gets its name from its call note, a complaining 'mew' like a cat." Still smiling, Cap looked inside the front cover of the book. He slammed it shut and handed it back to Jessie with a cross look on his face.

Jessie waited until Cap went back to his own reading to look at the inside page. She almost wished she hadn't. The words were written in a childish scrawl: "This book belongs to Jason Lambert." It brought tears to her eyes to think that Cap had a son who was no longer his friend.

Benny chattered steadily on the way to town, but Henry only half listened. Violet and Jessie had written down their grocery list, but he wasn't sure what *he* needed until he asked someone. He had a plan. He only hoped that what he wanted to do was possible. He was grateful that their grandfather always gave them enough money.

"That's the grocery store up ahead," Benny said.

"First we call home," Henry told him.

Mrs. McGregor answered on the third ring and laughed when she heard Henry's voice. "I told your grandfather you'd get in touch," she said. "He's going to call back tonight. Do you want me to give him any messages?"

"Only that we love him and we're all fine," he said. "And Benny sends his love to Watch."

"Tell him Watch is fine and loves him, too."

Benny beamed. "Now the grocery store?" he asked.

"Now the hardware store," Henry told him. "You like hardware stores, too, remember?"

"Maybe a little," Benny admitted.

Once he explained his plan, the woman who waited on Henry knew right away what he needed. "Is there a light fixture on the porch you described?" she asked.

Henry told her there was only an electrical outlet under the window. Then she brought him a floodlight with a heavy-duty extension cord. "You'll need to fasten the cord against the house so it won't whip in the wind. And this bracket to rest the floodlight in. Does Cap have a fox after his hens?"

Henry nodded. "My sister saw one this

morning. Cap thinks he might have a hawk or an eagle, too," he said.

She nodded. "This light will scare off any of those."

"Now the grocery store," Henry told Benny, grinning. Then he touched Benny's arm. Benny looked at him and then in the direction Henry was looking.

"There's that Mr. Jay again," Benny whispered. "Why isn't he back on the ship where he belongs?"

"I wonder about that myself," Henry said. "The minute I looked at him, he turned and went away fast. It really puzzles me the way he always does that."

Benny nooded. "Me, too. Maybe he can't stand our looks."

A bell rang over the door of the grocery store. The grocer beamed at them. "Our strangers are back. I hope you found Cap Lambert all right?"

"He's still on crutches, but he's fine," Benny said. "He has the greatest rooster in the whole world."

The grocer laughed and started reaching for the things on the girls' list. "That's for certain. Doodle's a beauty. Which size do you want of this canned ham?"

"The biggest one," Henry said. "We all like to eat." Since the man was so friendly, Henry asked him Benny's question. "We saw one of the men from our riverboat out there. We wondered why he's still around town instead of back on the boat."

"That is peculiar, isn't it?" the grocer agreed, filling a little bag with sunflower seeds. "But I know the man you mean. He's been around town for days. I never see him with anyone or talking to people. He reminds me of somebody, but I can't figure out who. He's not a very friendly fellow."

He handed Benny the sunflower seeds. "Here," he said. "These are for Cap's old rooster. Give them both my best."

CHAPTER 8

The Carpenter

"Nothing new in town, I guess," Cap said when the boys had brought in the groceries and brushed Pilot down.

"The new thing is going to be here," Henry told him.

Cap listened to him explain about putting up the floodlight and examined it carefully. "That's a clever way to drive away varmints. That's the biggest light I ever saw. Where did you think to put it up?"

"It should light both the chicken yard and the barn."

Cap nodded. "For that, it should be fastened at the back corner of the porch. You'll need a mighty long cord."

Henry nodded. "I bought the longest one, but let's check it anyway." Violet held the plug end of the cord next to the outlet. Jessie and Benny led the cord up the wall and out of the window. Henry, on the ladder at the corner of the porch, nodded when Jessie handed him the end. "It's going to work fine," Henry said. "There's even some extra."

Benny, on the ladder, handed the nails and hammer up as Henry fastened the metal bracket to the outside corner of the porch. Cap watched as Jessie and Violet hammered in the U-shaped nails to hold the cord against the wall.

"I don't know why I never thought of that," Cap said as Henry set the big floodlight into the bracket. "Now I can't wait until night to see how well it works."

When Cap returned to the front porch with Doodle on his shoulder, Jessie turned to Henry. "Now for the barn floor?"

Henry slapped his forehead with his hand. "Jessie! I can't believe this. I forgot to buy any extra nails."

"We could ask Cap if he has some," Violet suggested.

Jessie shook her head. "We need too many to explain to Cap. Let's see if we can't find some for ourselves."

The search for nails went slowly. They found a few bent ones in a toolbox in the barn. Benny went up in the loft to look. "Do you need a little red wagon?" he called down.

Henry laughed. "Not that I know of, why?"

"Because there's one up here," Benny told him. "And a box of books with all kinds of good pictures in them."

"How about nails?" Henry asked.

"Oh, I almost forgot," Benny said. He came down the ladder carrying a tin coffee can full of more bent nails.

"We'll hammer them straight on a flat rock

in the woods," Henry said. "That way Cap won't hear the noise."

"Somebody has to stay with Cap," Jessie said. "He gets nervous when we're gone too long. He was really fretting when Violet and I finally got back from the orchard today."

"Oh," Violet cried. "We haven't had a chance to tell you about the holes in the orchard."

"In the orchard!" Henry said. "Tell me about them while we straighten these nails."

While the others went to the woods, Jessie stayed with Cap. He cocked his head. "Do I hear hammering?" he asked.

Jessie nodded. "Henry's nailing down some loose boards in the barn," she said. "He really likes to stay busy."

"I've never seen such kids for work," he said.

As the hammering stopped, a low eerie cry sounded from high up in a pine tree. Jessie caught her breath. She thought of that awful whistling sound they had all heard. Though this was different, it was scary enough to make her shiver. Cap leaned to peer up into the tree. "Listen to that screech owl. Doesn't he make your blood run cold?"

"He sure does," Jessie said, laughing at how scared she'd been. "Your birds do make some strange noises!"

Henry and Benny came back from the barn. "I heard a spook or something out there," Benny cried.

Cap laughed. "That's the owl this glen is named for. There's nothing like a screech owl to raise your hair up. It makes some people think this place is haunted." Seeing Benny's eyes widen, Cap changed the subject. "I'm glad you boys are back," he said, reaching for his crutches. "I've been smelling that applesauce all day, and I say it's time to eat."

Henry nodded and glanced at his sister. The screech owl *had* made a scary noise, but it hadn't "raised his hair up" as badly as that awful whistle they had all heard at one time or another. But he couldn't believe Cap's cabin was haunted . . . by what?

At the table Cap turned to Henry. "So

now you're a carpenter," he said. "Did you get the barn back in shape?"

Henry nodded. "I like carpenter work."

"I sure appreciate all you're doing," Cap said, reaching for the bowl to take another serving of applesauce.

"And I appreciate applesauce," Benny said, taking the bowl from Cap to serve himself again.

That night before going to bed, they turned on the big new floodlight. The yard and barn were almost as bright as day.

Jessie had heard the scary whistling sound the first night they spent in Cap's cabin. She and Henry and Benny had all seen the flickering light. Benny had kept talking about a strange scraping sound. Later Henry had heard the whistling, and Violet had heard it the morning she saw the strange creature running off into the dark woods.

After Henry put up the big floodlight, everything stopped. For several days there was no strange whistling sound, no light, no scraping sound, and no more sign of the awkward dark creature that Violet had seen.

Henry was puzzled. "Did we imagine all that stuff?" he asked.

"That can't be it," Violet told him. "The holes were real, and Cap talked to me about that whistling."

"Maybe that strange creature got scared when Violet saw it out by the barn that morning," Jessie suggested.

"Or maybe it's been afraid to come back since you put that floodlight up," Violet said.

"Oh, I don't like those ideas at all," Benny said.

The others stared at him. "Why not?"

He shrugged. "That would mean we haven't helped Cap at all. Those things could come back and scare Cap again, or make him have another accident after we're gone."

Jessie sighed. "Benny hit the nail on the head again," she said. "What's more, this trip was only supposed to last ten days. We only have about three days left."

"Maybe Grandfather will be too busy to

come get us on time," Violet said hopefully.

"Grandfather *always* keeps promises," Benny told them.

The mailman hadn't stopped at Cap's cabin once since the children came. The very next day he stopped out in the road and tooted his horn twice. Cap looked up in surprise. "That's a change," he said. "I don't get much mail. You boys want to run and get it for me?"

After Henry took the letter, Benny carried it back to Cap on the porch. "How's the old man doing?" the mailman asked Henry. "I was sorry to hear about his fall."

"He's getting better every day," Henry told him.

"I thought about stopping but I always run late. Then when I saw that he had help out here, I quit worrying."

"You mean us?" Henry asked. He hadn't thought of them as "help," but he liked the way that sounded.

The mailman shrugged. "Maybe I'm wrong. I keep seeing a strange man on the road. I thought he worked for Cap."

Henry frowned. "What does this man look like?"

"Sober fellow, never smiles," the mailman said. As he described the man, Henry caught a quick breath. The mailman was describing Mr. Jay from the riverboat perfectly.

"Tell Cap to get well soon," the mailman added, putting his car in gear and starting off. Henry walked back to the porch thoughtfully. It was one thing for Mr. Jay to hang around town and act strange, but hearing that he was walking up and down Cap's road really bothered Henry.

Cap's letter was from Mr. Alden. He read it aloud. Grandfather Alden had gotten the children's message from Mrs. McGregor and appreciated hearing from them. He told Cap not to worry about the kids, that they were doing what they liked to do best. He said to expect him this coming Saturday. He was eager to see all of them.

"We need to fix a good fancy meal for my old friend," Cap said. "You probably need to ride Pilot into town again. I'd hate not to give your grandfather a hearty welcome."

"We could use a few things," Jessie said. "Maybe we could go tomorrow. That would leave us time for other jobs."

"What other jobs?" Cap asked. "You've done plenty!"

Violet grinned at him. "Oh, Cap," she said. "Even though your ankle is ever so much better, you'll still have to use that cane for a while. We've thought of lots of little things to help with before we leave." She didn't add what she was really thinking — that they meant to solve the mysteries before they went off and left him alone.

"Like climb the trees and pick the apples," Benny said.

"And weed and thin the garden," Violet put in.

"And I'd like to clean up the barn," Henry said. "I want to sweep up the loose hay to save it for Pilot."

Cap threw up his hands. "I give up," he said. "But groceries for your grandfather's dinner come first. Agreed?"

CHAPTER 9

Storm Clouds

"We need a really good grocery list," Jessie told the others. "Cap wants Grandfather's dinner to be special."

"And it's our last chance to cook for Cap," Henry added. Everyone wanted to add something. It was late when they finally finished the list and went to bed.

They were barely asleep when the wind rose. Before Jessie and Henry could even get the windows closed, a cold rain came blowing in, too. Lightning sliced across the sky, followed by crashing thunder.

"Come on, Henry," Jessie cried, pulling the yellow oilskin ponchos from the hooks by the door. "I'll check the chicken house windows. You check on Pilot."

Leaning into the driving rain, Jessie ran to the henhouse while Henry closed the windows and doors of the barn. Violet and Benny were huddled together under a dry blanket watching the storm when they got back inside. The thunder had wakened Cap. He stood in the door, frowning. "You kids all right? Not scared, are you?"

Violet shook her head. "It's beautiful," she said.

The thunder finally growled away, but the rain kept coming. It settled into a slow steady drumming against the closed porch windows. It was still falling the next morning.

"We're stuck here today," Cap told them. "Possum Creek is probably up over our road."

Violet made hot biscuits to eat with honey and scrambled eggs. "Maybe you'd like some of that canned ham with these biscuits," Cap suggested.

"Let's save it for when Grandfather comes," Jessie said. "In case the storm keeps us from getting to town."

Since they couldn't work outside, the children cleaned the inside of Cap's windows. After supper they made a hearth fire and roasted marshmallows until Cap went off to bed.

Henry went out to check on Pilot one last time. He came back within minutes, his poncho dripping. Jessie could tell from his face that he was upset. He motioned to the others to gather close. "Somebody's been out there since I shut the barn up. One of the windows I had closed was open, and hay was scattered all over the barn floor again."

"The wind could have done that," Violet said, looking thoughtful. "Did you turn on the lights and look around?"

Henry shook his head. "I was afraid Cap would see them from his bedroom window."

"I know where there's a big flashlight," Benny said. "I found it when I was straightening some shelves."

Jessie reached for her shoes. "That's wonderful. Let's go out with the flashlight."

"That's a good idea," Violet said. "We need to find an answer, even if it's only the wind."

"Do we all have to go?" Henry asked, looking at Benny.

"Don't even think about leaving me here," Benny told him. "After all, I'm the one who found the flashlight."

Since they had only two ponchos, the children doubled up in them. They made their way to the barn between great puddles of rain. Henry stopped outside of the window he had found open. "There," he said, shining the flashlight on the ground. "Footsteps, right in the mud."

"Are you sure they're not yours?" Violet asked.

"Positive," Henry said, holding up his boot. "See, my soles are smooth, and these have a waffle weave on them."

There were more waffle-weave footsteps inside the barn. The children looked at each other. "Why would anyone want to poke

around out here during such a storm?" Jessie asked.

"Maybe they felt safe because the flood-light was off," Henry suggested.

"And we couldn't hear them for the thunder," Benny added.

"But why do they come here at all? Why are they doing this? They *can't* just be trying to scare Cap!" Violet said.

Jessie kicked some hay aside to clear a path. "Look, Henry," she said. "Here's a hole with a loose board over it that you missed."

He knelt beside her and shook his head. "I didn't miss it," he said. "It's been pried up again. See that old rusty nail I used to fasten it down?"

Violet was walking past Pilot's stall when she stopped and stood frowning. "What's wrong?" Benny asked her.

"It smells funny in here," she said. "Not like wet hay and horses, but a sharp kind of smell."

Henry sniffed and nodded. "That's kerosene," he said. "You know, the liquid they burn in lamps. I know the barn didn't smell like that when I was in here before."

"It's dangerous to have that kind of lamp around all this loose hay," Jessie said. "It could start a fire."

"Lamp," Violet cried. "Remember that funny flickering light we saw? If it had been a flashlight, someone would have pointed it ahead and up and down. But a lamp . . ."

"You're right," Henry said. "You carry a lamp with a handle that goes over the top. It would always be at about the same height. It would also *seem* to flicker when you went behind a tree or a fence post."

Jessie sat down on an overturned bucket with her chin in her hands. "Who *could* be coming here to stamp around in the mud, carrying a lamp?"

"Or to dig holes in the barn and orchard," Benny added.

"Or to pick vegetables and steal a chicken and eggs?" Violet reminded them.

"We need two things, a who and a why," Jessie said.

"If we could find out *who* it was, we'd

probably know the why," Henry told her.

Benny stood very still, thinking. "Do you remember what Mr. Edwards said about the pirates lying in wait to grab people?" he asked dreamily. "Couldn't we do that? Then we'd grab the who, and make them tell us the why."

Henry stared at Benny, then laughed softly. "There's our Benny, figuring out exactly what needs to be done."

"The hayloft," Benny went on. "If we were hidden in the hayloft, we could see anyone who came in down here."

"Nobody's said *anything* about that strange scary whistling noise," Violet reminded them. "Could that be some kind of a signal? If so, maybe there are at least two people in this gang."

"Now we're getting somewhere," Henry said. "We need to make a plan. Let's go back to the cabin and figure out exactly what to do."

"The door," Benny whispered. "I just heard a door bang at the cabin." When they rushed to the barn window to look out, they saw Cap in his white nightshirt leaning on his cane in the clearing. Then the awful whistle sounded from the direction of the orchard. It was dark in the shadow of the barn, but they could see a bulky shadow leaping away into the trees.

Violet gasped. "There it is again. That's the same thing I saw running away when I was in the henhouse."

"The dwarf," Benny whispered. As they spoke, Cap turned and walked back toward the cabin.

"But now we do know something for sure," Henry said. "There have to be at least two people. One person stands guard and whistles to the other one as a warning."

"Let's go figure out what to do," Jessie said, shivering. "I can't believe that they'll dare come back tonight."

CHAPTER 10

Henry's Plan

That night they talked a long time. They went over their plan until each of them knew exactly what to do. They talked so late that Thursday morning came too fast.

Again the sky was dark and overcast. As they sat down for breakfast, Cap said, "Not much of a night for sleeping, was it?"

Henry was flipping golden brown pancakes in an iron skillet. Violet carried them to the table on warmed plates.

"Did you have trouble sleeping?" Benny asked Cap.

"Some," he said. "How about you?"

"When I did sleep, I did it good," Benny told him.

"Then nobody heard any animals crashing around or strange cries or anything?" Cap asked.

Violet put her fork down and looked up at him. "Well . . ." she began.

Jessie interrupted her quietly. "Come on, Violet, let's do the dishes since Henry cooked."

"I felt terrible at breakfast," Violet told Jessie. "Ever since we've been here, we've done nothing but keep secrets from Cap. It makes me feel dishonest."

Jessie nodded. "I feel the same way, but it's almost over. If we can catch the people who are making him so nervous, keeping secrets from him will be worth it."

When the sun still hadn't come out by afternoon, Cap shook his head. "At this rate, you won't be able to get to town on Pilot tomorrow, either. I don't know what we're going to feed your grandfather on Saturday."

"We'll do fine if we can get into the garden tomorrow," Violet said. "But it's probably pure mud out there now."

"Worse comes to worse, I can tell you how to build bridges into the garden," Cap told her.

"Grandfather will be able to get here without building bridges, won't he?" Benny asked Cap with a worried look.

The old man nodded. "He'll have no problem in one of those big cars he always rents. It's not like having a horse loaded with four kids and a bunch of groceries." He glanced around. "Is that Henry back out at the barn again? Pilot's going to be lonesome when that boy leaves."

Jessie knew what Henry was doing out there with Pilot. He was fixing the barn lights so that all of them could be turned on with a single switch just inside Pilot's stall. She was really proud of the plan they had worked out. And they had all gone over it so many times the night before that she was positive it would work.

Every single one of them had a different job. Jessie herself would be the lookout in the hayloft. She would have the flashlight. The minute she saw anyone creeping into the barn, she would wink the flashlight three times out of the window of the loft.

Benny was to stay on the back porch and keep watching to see her signal from the hayloft window. The minute he saw Jessie flash the light three times, he would switch on the floodlight and make the whole barnyard as bright as day.

Violet would be standing inside the barn, just inside Pilot's stall where she could reach the switch Henry had fixed. When she saw the lights go on outside, she would turn on all the lights inside the barn. Whoever tried to come in there would be covered with light from both inside and out of the barn.

Henry was to stand just inside the chicken yard fence. He got that job because he was the biggest and the fastest runner. He would leave the gate open a little bit so that he could get out and start running fast. He would race across the yard and slam the barn door and lock the prowler inside. That way he couldn't run away before they caught him.

Everything *had* to work perfectly.

That was the longest day ever. When dinnertime finally came, nobody was even hungry. "You kids *must* be excited to see your grandfather," Cap said when Benny turned down a second helping of spaghetti.

Finally, it felt strange to be in bed fully dressed except for their shoes. They hardly breathed waiting for Henry to decide it was time to go out and take their places.

"It's so noisy tonight," Benny whispered.

"It sounds that way because we're being so quiet," Jessie told him. But it was noisy. The frogs croaked. Off in the woods, the screech owl gave its trembling eerie call, sending a shiver up everyone's spine.

Henry watched the moon climb up the overcast sky. Mostly it was only behind the clouds. Once in a while, it broke free and flooded the wet barn and the yard around it with a silvery light.

Jessie was watching, too. "Look how

plainly you can see everything in that light."

Henry nodded. "We should go as soon as the moon gets hidden behind that big bank of clouds."

The minute the moon slid under the clouds, Violet and Jessie went outside. They stood in the shadows of the cabin only a minute before making a dash for the barn door which Henry had left open for them.

"Is your heart beating like everything?" Violet asked Jessie when they were safe inside the barn and Jessie was starting up into the loft.

Jessie nodded. "I don't like to think I'm afraid, but my skin feels creepy, too."

"I'm scared and I know it," Violet told her.

Jessie felt her way carefully up the wooden ladder into the loft. With the flashlight in her hand, she crept through the dark to the high window.

When Violet let herself inside the stall where Pilot stood, the big horse stamped his foot, then whinnied softly. After she had located the light switch, Violet stroked Pilot's long warm head.

Back on the porch, Henry and Benny watched the girls make their shadowy run across the open yard. "Now it's my turn," Henry told Benny. "Whatever you do, don't get sleepy."

"I'm already sleepy," Benny told him, "but that doesn't mean I'll go to sleep. I've even practiced pinching myself to stay awake."

When the moon disappeared again, Henry made his way to the chicken yard and stood by the tall post just inside the gate.

The moon continued to rise in the sky as the time passed. Henry worried about Benny, back on the porch, pinching himself to stay awake. He even worried that the prowlers might not come at all.

He leaned against the fence post and sighed. This wasn't the first mystery they had been involved in, but it was the most puzzling. Even if he hadn't liked Cap Lambert as much as he did, it was terrible for someone to be scaring an old man. The plan *had* to work.

Suddenly something caught his eye.

Something or someone smaller than a man, all dressed in dark clothing, was creeping around the side of the barn, moving awkwardly.

He drew in his breath and held it. How strangely the creature walked, unevenly, as if it were dragging something heavy at its side. Then the dark creature melted into the shadow of the barn, and Henry let his breath out slowly.

In a minute it would be inside the barn. In a minute he would see Jessie's signal from the barn loft. He had to be ready to run faster then he had ever run in his whole life.

CHAPTER 11

The Hayloft

Henry watched the barn loft for Jessie's signal. He pushed the chicken yard gate open a little wider so he could make a faster getaway.

Just as he saw the three quick blinks of light at the loft window, something shot past him through the open gate to the hen yard, almost throwing him off balance.

At least Benny had not gone to sleep. As Henry got his balance and raced madly toward the barn door, lights seemed to come from everywhere. The barnyard was as brightly lit as daytime, and the barn itself looked lit up for a party.

But the small dark figure Henry had seen creeping into the barn only moments before was getting away. It had stepped into the barn and right back out through the barn door that he was supposed to have slammed shut. Now it raced toward the orchard.

He had failed.

He hadn't managed to get to the barn door in time. As he bolted after the escaping figure, paying no attention to where he was going, he tripped on something that made a loud metallic noise. He fell to the ground with a yell of pain. As he tried to get up, he found himself tangled in a heavy woven bag.

A shovel. The thief had been dragging a heavy shovel and that bag along behind him. No wonder he had walked that strange way. But of course he had to have some heavy tool to dig all those holes. The shovel scraping against the rocks in the ground must have caused "that scraping sound" Benny had heard.

As Henry leaped to his feet, Violet sped

past him, rapidly gaining on the running figure. The whistling warning signal came from
somewhere in the orchard, but too late.
Henry and Violet caught up with the runner
at about the same moment. All three of them
went down together in a pile, rolling over
and over on the muddy ground. Henry got
to his feet first and grabbed the thief with
both arms. He still didn't know what he had
caught. It was wearing a dark mask and a
black hood over its head. It kicked and beat
at Henry with its fists as he took it back
toward the barnyard.

Once there, he shoved it against the side
of the barn, and tried to pin back its arms.

He was hearing all sorts of astonishing
things at once. Benny was yelling and crying
out, "Take that! Get going!" at the top of his
lungs while Jessie and Violet danced around
Henry, trying to help but not knowing how
to.

Even Cap, in his white nightshirt, was
coming, with a crutch in one hand and his
cane in the other.

"Pull his mask off," Henry shouted at Jessie. "I don't dare let him go a minute."

Just as Jessie got a firm grip on the mask, Cap came up behind her, breathing heavily. With a final jerk, Jessie managed to get the dark fabric loose. Jessie gasped. A tumble of bright curls fell on the shoulder of the robe, and a young girl's terrified face looked back into hers.

"Susie," Cap cried out in shock.

Susie Hodges looked up at Cap, covered her face with her hands, and began to sob bitterly. Violet went past Jessie to put her arms around the girl. "There," she said. "Don't cry. Nobody's going to hurt you."

Cap reached for the girl's hand. "Violet's right, Susie. We're not going to hurt you. But I don't understand what's going on."

When his words only started a fresh flood of tears, Violet took the girl's hand and turned to Cap. "Maybe if we all went inside out of the damp air, then she'd feel better."

Susie shook her head fiercely. "No, I can't. Ned."

"Where is your little brother?" Jessie asked gently.

"Out there," Susie said, nodding toward the orchard.

"Did he make that warning whistle?" Henry asked.

When she nodded, Cap's voice turned gruff. "That's enough. I want explanations, not this nonsense. Susie, call Ned, and both of you come inside my cabin this very minute."

Susie looked at him, her damp face tearful, then called her brother's name. He walked forward slowly, a small fair-haired boy with blue eyes and freckles. When Susie put out her hand, he seized it gratefully.

Cap hobbled along ahead. He led all the children into the house and glanced at the clock. "Two o'clock in the morning," he snorted. "I don't know what this world is coming to."

Benny stared at Susie. "Boy, you sure aren't any ghost. I was afraid this place was haunted."

Susie, her head in her hands, sat trembling on a chair by the fireplace with Ned on the floor by her feet. When Jessie started off into the kitchen, Cap crossly asked her where she thought she was going.

"To make some hot cocoa," she said, ignoring his gruff tone.

He hesitated, then nodded as he turned back to the rest of the children. "Where should we begin?"

"With the holes in the barn," Benny suggested. "I fell on a board that had been pulled up from the floor of the barn, and there was a hole dug under it."

At Cap's startled look, Henry took over. He told about the whistling noise and Benny hearing scraping.

"And the strange light we saw from the porch that first night," Violet added. "You told us how you hadn't been able to do your work," she reminded him. "But there weren't as many eggs as there should have been, and the garden had been picked. No rotten vegetables or fruit anywhere."

"We were hungry," Susie wailed. "It was going to waste."

"My prize Rhode Island red chicken, too?" Cap asked, suddenly sounding angry again.

"We never took a chicken, not ever," Ned said. "Just some eggs that weren't being gathered. And we fed the chickens, too, didn't we, Susie?"

"You see, Cap," Jessie broke in. "It was all too mysterious. Finally we set a trap for the thieves."

"We're not thieves," Susie said, glaring at her. "We were only trying to help Mother."

"Did you make those awful whistling noises in the woods, Ned?" Cap asked. When the little boy nodded, he turned to Susie. "What about the strange lights?"

"We carried a kerosene lantern to see by and we dressed all in black so no one could see us."

"And the scraping sound?" Benny asked.

"I could only find a really heavy shovel. I had to drag it along with the bag I carried."

"You've already explained the vegetables and the eggs, but why in the world would you tear up my barn floor and dig holes all over my place?"

Susie looked down so that her words came out muffled. "That's what the bag was for.

We were looking for buried pirate treasure. I read about it being hidden here, and we needed the money so very badly."

Jessie came in with cups of cocoa. She stopped in front of Susie and frowned. "Did you read this article about buried pirate gold in your newspaper?"

Susie nodded. "This man wrote that a lot of pirate treasure was supposed to be hidden right here in Owl's Glen around an old cabin that had been here for a hundred years. Cap's cabin was the only one like that."

The Alden children looked at each other. Paul Edwards would feel terrible if he knew how much trouble his words had caused. What had he said to them on the boat? "Stories of buried treasure never seem to die away, but nobody ever finds any gold, either."

CHAPTER 12

The Real Treasure

Cap's voice was gentle again as he turned to Susie and her brother. "Does your mother know about this treasure hunt of yours?"

"Oh, no," Susie cried, her eyes wide with fright. "She would never let us do it. She must never find out. But we simply had to help her. After Daddy died, our money ran out right away. She tried everywhere to find work, but she only knows how to take care of people and cook wonderful food."

"Where is she now while you kids are out gallivanting in the middle of the night like this?" Cap asked.

"She sits with old Granny Smothers, who can't stay nights alone. But she's poor, too. She can only pay Mother enough money to meet the mortgage. Ned and I thought . . ."

"Didn't you and Ned ever think of coming to your friends?" Cap asked crossly. "Didn't you know that we loved you and would help if we knew you needed it?"

"Please don't fuss at Susie," Violet said. "When our mother and father died, we didn't think of going to friends, either. We just found the boxcar and set out to take care of ourselves."

Cap grinned and put his arm around Susie. "Of course you're right. I didn't mean to be cross. It's just that I feel so bad that you went hungry and worked so hard and all for nothing."

"I'm really sorry about the vegetables and the eggs," Susie said.

"And the chicken?" Cap asked again.

"We *didn't* take any chicken," Ned repeated.

"Forget the chicken then," Cap said, leaning toward Susie and Ned. "Let me tell you about those stories of pirate gold. They are like fairy stories, fun to think about but dangerous to believe in. But there *is* treasure in this neighborhood, Susie, real genuine treasure."

Her blue eyes stared at him in wonder as he took her hands. "Our real treasure is the love we have for each other." As Susie dropped her eyes, he shook his head. "I treasure you children and your mother above all the gold in this world. I can prove it."

The room was completely still as all the children stared at him. "Do you know what I need more than anything? It's somebody to keep this cabin clean and fix me healthy hot food the way these children have. To listen to my stories and tell me theirs, and make me laugh. Susie, these children are going back home Saturday. I want you to ask your mother if she would take a job with me. I'd pay handsomely to have the rest of my days as happy and comfortable as the last week has been."

"Cap," Violet cried, running to hug him. "What a wonderful idea. Would she do that, Susie? Would your mother do that?"

"I'm sure she would," Susie said. "She likes taking care of people more than anything in the world."

The tiniest tinge of light was showing over the woods when Susie and Ned left for home. As Benny stood at the door, watching them leave, he looked up at Cap. "Doesn't anyone want to hear about me and the fox?" he asked.

"What fox?" Cap looked down at him, confused.

"The one that ran into the chicken yard just as I turned the floodlight on."

The girls sprang to their feet and would have started right out to the chicken house but Benny stopped them. "He's gone now. I ran after him and threw rocks," he explained. "He snapped at me but he kept on running."

Henry stared at Benny with his mouth open, remembering that something had brushed by him just as he saw Jessie's signal. And Benny's shouts while Henry was pinning Susie to the wall. "Take that," Benny had been yelling. "Get going!"

"Did you beat him to the chickens?" Cap asked, grinning.

Benny nodded. "They were all flapping around on the ceiling when I went in. I drove him off before he caught any. And I locked them up safe, too. He smelled bad anyway."

Cap leaned on his cane as he rose from his chair. "I hope you children haven't any more excitement up your sleeves for me. I've just about had my share for this year and the next one coming."

As Jessie undressed for bed, she thought about their mystery man, Mr. Jay. Maybe it was just as well they had never mentioned him to Cap. But she still wondered why he had been walking up and down Cap's road, and why he always seemed to be spying on them and was so unfriendly.

That next day went all too quickly. Jessie suggested that they not even try to ride Pilot into town. "You know how much fun it is to make do with what we've got."

Mrs. Hodges came with Susie and Ned right after lunch. She looked very unhappy when she came, but when she and Cap and the children finished talking in the living room, she was smiling.

Susie and Ned sat on the back porch drinking lemonade with the Alden children.

"The thing we hate the most is that Cap fell in that hole of ours and got hurt," Ned said quietly.

"He's fine now," Violet reminded him. "It isn't like he broke a bone or anything."

By the time they left, everyone was tired. "Is that grandfather of ours ever going to get here?" Benny asked as he tumbled into bed with his eyes already half shut.

"Tomorrow," Violet said.

CHAPTER 13

The Final Surprise

When Cap, with only a cane for support, came to the kitchen door, he laughed. "Look at you! The sun's barely up, and you already have breakfast started. Where are the boys?"

"Henry's out taking care of Pilot, and Benny is gathering eggs," Jessie told him. "Grandfather could get here early, and we want to be ready."

"That's right," Cap said. "This is the day of the big party, isn't it?"

"A really big party!" Violet said. "Grand-

father, and Mrs. Hodges, and Susie and Ned
all at once. Won't it be fun?"

"I guess I don't even know what we're
going to eat," Cap said, looking around the
kitchen. "You never did get to take that shop-
ping trip into town."

Jessie laughed. "We didn't need any grocery store. And dinner today is going to be
a surprise. You do like surprises, don't you?"

Cap laughed. "If I didn't before, I've
learned to this past week. I've sure had
enough of them since you came."

Benny was the first to see his grandfather
coming. He was in the chicken yard when
he saw the long black car pull up in front
of the cabin. He went flying around the
house without even thinking to close the
gate.

First there were hugs all around, then the
children had to take their grandfather for a
tour of the barn and garden and orchard.
Finally he joined Cap on the front porch,
talking over old times.

All four of the children were working on
their special meal when Benny looked out

the porch window and began to yell. They crowded around him to see why he was so excited.

Violet, still wearing her long apron, ran to the front porch. "Oh, Cap, Grandfather," she shouted. "Come and see what's happening out in back."

As the men came around the side of the house, they saw a huge red hen walking out of the woods, clucking happily. Behind her came about a dozen little chicks, peeping and scratching their way toward the gate of the hen yard that Benny had left open.

"Rhoda!" Cap cried. "Doodle, look at that! We'd given up our good friend Rhoda for lost. Now she's come home!"

Jessie asked, "Where do you suppose they've been?"

Cap laughed. "Rhoda has always had a mind of her own. She must have gotten out about the time I was hurt and made her nest in the woods. She's lucky that a fox or a hawk didn't get her or those babies."

Mr. Alden looked at his old friend a moment. "Do you mean that you're going to

welcome her back even though she went off the way she did?"

Cap stared at him. "Of course," he said. "She was only following her own nature like any creature would."

"*People* do that, too," Mr. Alden reminded him, his voice suddenly very quiet.

Cap stared at him. "I'm not sure I know what you're getting at, but you sound mighty serious."

Mr. Alden took Cap's arm and led him back to the porch. "Don't you?" he asked. "I'm talking about your son, Jason, that's what. He and I have been writing letters back and forth for almost a year. He wants to come home in the worst way but has been afraid to. He wasn't sure he'd be welcome."

Cap fell silent, staring at his hands. "He's welcome," he said gruffly. "I've never quit missing him. It's been even worse since I've had your grandchildren here. But I don't even know where he is."

"He's at the hotel in town," Mr. Alden told him. "I talked to him just this morning. When he heard you were hurt, he tried to call you but didn't have the nerve to talk."

"That was Jason breathing on my phone?" Cap asked.

Mr. Alden nodded. "He left his ship when the children came. But he didn't know how to make peace with you."

"There's no peace to make," Cap said crossly. "He was young and stubborn and I was older and stubborn. That's long years ago now. I want to see my boy!"

Mr. Alden rose and called into the house. "How long until dinner's ready, Jessie?"

"About a half hour," she called. "Is that too long?"

"It's perfect," her grandfather said. "Tell Violet to set another plate. Cap and I are going to town, but we'll be right back with one more guest."

Violet had set the table with a white cloth and a great bowl of wild blue larkspur in the center. "It's the closest I could find to a violet color," she said wistfully.

The Hodges family arrived right away. Benny had taken Susie and Ned out to see the new baby chickens when the big black car returned. Jessie watched from the window as her grandfather got out, helped Cap out, and handed him his cane. Then she gasped. "Violet! Henry!" she called. "Our mystery man, Mr. Jay, is here. I don't believe this."

Then Cap called, "Hey, children, come meet my son."

"Jason," Henry whispered. "Mr. Jay is really Jason."

Now Cap's son smiled, a broad sweet smile that was a little bit like Cap's. "We've met," he said, shaking hands with each of them. "We even traveled together, didn't we?"

The children nodded and glanced at their grandfather.

"Jason was pretty envious that you children were coming to where he wanted to be," their grandfather said.

"Well, he's here now," Violet said with a smile. "And as welcome as can be!" Her eyes flew wide open. "Jessie," she squealed. "Do I smell something burning?" The two girls flew off to the kitchen. But within a minute Violet was back.

"Just one thing, Mr. Jay," she said. "If you knew who we were and that we were coming here, why were you so unfriendly? Every time we saw you, you just turned your back and hurried away like you couldn't stand the sight of us."

"I'm not Mr. Jay to you, Violet, I'm just Jason. And the reason I turned away was that I didn't know what my father looked like anymore. For all I knew, you might have recognized that we were father and son." He grinned and tugged lightly at his father's beard. "If I had known about this bush he is wearing, I wouldn't have acted like that."

Cap laughed right along with Violet and the others.

Benny was the last one to meet Jason Lambert. He sighed, put his hand in his pocket, and pulled out the little fire engine he had found in the tree house.

"This is yours," he said quietly.

Jason lifted the little metal toy and looked at it carefully. Then he placed it back in

Benny's palm. "I believe you're right, Benny," he said. "And I'm glad to have it. It's the perfect present for me to give you. Would you like to keep it to remember Owl's Glen by?"

Benny smiled and closed his fingers around the tiny toy. "Oh, yes," he cried.

The meal was beautiful. The canned ham was glazed with rings of apples dyed red with cinnamon candies. Tiny new potatoes swam in butter beside a bowl of ruby-red beets.

Mrs. Hodges finally put down her fork with a sigh. "What a wonderful meal," she said.

"And every single thing except the canned ham is from Cap's garden and orchard," Jessie told her.

"We have dessert, too," Benny said.

"I don't know where I'll find room for it," Jason said.

Cap took a spoonful of Violet's apple bread pudding with caramel sauce and grinned at his son. "Don't even try to eat this, Jason," he said. "Just pass it right over here. One serving of this isn't going to be near enough for me."

"You and I are a lot alike, Cap," Benny said, smiling at him. "We both like good things in our mouths, don't we?"

The grown-ups sat over coffee while the children cleaned up the dishes, then played games in the backyard. Before they left, Mrs. Hodges asked Violet for her recipe for apple bread pudding and caramel sauce. "It's just delicious," she told Violet. "I'll want to make it for Cap to remind him of you. I just wish you could stay."

"We might come back," Benny said. "I like it here."

As Mr. Alden's car pulled away, Cap waved back with his rooster on his shoulder and his son at his side. "This may have been our best mystery adventure ever," Jessie told her grandfather thoughtfully.

Benny said, "Yes, but I want to get home and see Watch and our boxcar."

Jessie grinned at him. Funny little boy. But Jessie knew Benny was only saying what each of them felt.

GERTRUDE CHANDLER WARNER discovered when she was teaching that many readers who like an exciting story could find no books that were both easy and fun to read. She decided to try to meet this need, and her first book, *The Boxcar Children*, quickly proved she had succeeded.

Miss Warner drew on her own experiences to write the mystery. As a child she spent hours watching trains go by on the tracks opposite her family home. She often dreamed about what it would be like to set up housekeeping in a caboose or freight car — the situation the Alden children find themselves in.

When Miss Warner received requests for more adventures involving Henry, Jessie, Violet, and Benny Alden, she began additional stories. In each, she chose a special setting and introduced unusual or eccentric characters who liked the unpredictable.

While the mystery element is central to each of Miss Warner's books, she never thought of them as strictly juvenile mysteries. She liked to stress the Aldens' independence and resourcefulness and their solid New England devotion to using up and making do. The Aldens go about most of their adventures with as little adult supervision as possible — something else that delights young readers.

Miss Warner lived in Putnam, Connecticut, until her death in 1979. During her lifetime, she received hundreds of letters from girls and boys telling her how much they liked her books.